"I'm always amazed and delighted by 'Bear Hunt'. I learnt it in the early eighties as a song for children to join in with. It's a chant, a poem, a fun-and-games romp with actions to make up and moments of shock and horror to giggle over. When I was asked to turn it into a story to be illustrated, I wondered if it was possible but I had a try, added some words of my own and waited. Then came the day I saw Helen Oxenbury's pictures – and I was utterly blown away. She had turned those words into a family epic: a set of difficulties that a father and his children face together in a landscape of depth, beauty and emotion. And when you look into the book, there are powerful feelings to explore: fear, worry, exultation and sympathy. After all, what is the bear thinking on the last page?"

Michael Rosen

For Geraldine, Joe, Naomi,
Eddie, Laura and Isaac
M.R.

For Amelia
H.O.

First published 1989 by Walker Books Ltd
87 Vauxhall Walk, London SE11 5HJ

This edition published 2014

10 9 8 7 6 5 4 3 2 1

Text © 1989 Michael Rosen
Illustrations © 1989 Helen Oxenbury

The right of Michael Rosen and Helen Oxenbury
to be identified as author and illustrator respectively
of this work has been asserted by them in accordance
with the Copyright, Designs and Patents Act 1988

This book has been typeset in Veronan Light Educational

Printed in China

British Library Cataloguing in Publication Data:
a catalogue record for this book is available from
the British Library

ISBN: 978-1-4063-5727-1

www.walker.co.uk

We're Going on a Bear Hunt
25TH ANNIVERSARY EDITION

Retold by
Michael Rosen

Illustrated by
Helen Oxenbury

WALKER BOOKS
AND SUBSIDIARIES
LONDON • BOSTON • SYDNEY • AUCKLAND

We're going on a bear hunt.

We're going to catch a big one.

What a beautiful day!

We're not scared.

Uh-uh! Grass!

Long wavy grass.

We can't go over it.

We can't go under it.

Oh no!

We've got to go through it!

Swishy swashy!
Swishy swashy!
Swishy swashy!

We're going on a bear hunt.

We're going to catch a big one.

What a beautiful day!

We're not scared.

Uh-uh! A river!

A deep cold river.

We can't go over it.

We can't go under it.

Oh no!

We've got to go through it!

Splash splosh!
Splash splosh!
Splash splosh!

We're going on a bear hunt.

We're going to catch a big one.

What a beautiful day!

We're not scared.

Uh-uh! Mud!

Thick oozy mud.

We can't go over it.

We can't go under it.

Oh no!

We've got to go through it!

Squelch squerch!
Squelch squerch!
Squelch squerch!

We're going on a bear hunt.

We're going to catch a big one.

What a beautiful day!

We're not scared.

Uh-uh! A forest!

A big dark forest.

We can't go over it.

We can't go under it.

Oh no!

We've got to go through it!

Stumble trip!
Stumble trip!
Stumble trip!

We're going on a bear hunt.

We're going to catch a big one.

What a beautiful day!

We're not scared.

Uh-uh! A snowstorm!

A swirling whirling snowstorm.

We can't go over it.

We can't go under it.

Oh no!

We've got to go through it!

Hoooo woooo!
Hoooo woooo!
Hoooo woooo!

We're going on a bear hunt.

We're going to catch a big one.

What a beautiful day!

We're not scared.

Uh-uh! A cave!

A narrow gloomy cave.

We can't go over it.

We can't go under it.

Oh no!

We've got to go through it!

Tiptoe!

Tiptoe!

Tiptoe!

WHAT'S THAT?

One shiny wet nose!

Two big furry ears!

Two big goggly eyes!

IT'S A BEAR!!!!

Quick! Back through the cave! Tiptoe! Tiptoe! Tiptoe!

Back through the snowstorm! Hoooo woooooo! Hoooo woooooo!

Back through the forest! Stumble trip! Stumble trip! Stumble trip!

Back through the mud! Squelch squerch! Squelch squerch!

Back through the river! Splash splosh! Splash splosh! Splash splosh!

Back through the grass! Swishy swashy! Swishy swashy!

Get to our front door.

Open the door.

Up the stairs.

Oh no!

We forgot to shut the door.

Back downstairs.

Shut the door.

Back upstairs.

Into the bedroom.

Into bed.

Under the covers.

We're not going on

a bear hunt again.